Heidi

Adapted from the Original Story by
JOHANNA SPYRI

Pictures by Corinne M...

gb GOLD...
Western Publ...
Racin...

Fourteenth Printing, 1978

This adaptation of Johanna Spyri's classic story *Heidi* has been especially illustrated for Golden Books by Corinne Malvern. Among Miss Malvern's other Little Golden Books are *How Big?* and *Frosty the Snowman*.

ON TOP of a mountain in the Swiss Alps, Heidi lived with her grandfather.

Their home was a hut overlooking the valley, and behind it stood three old fir trees. Heidi loved to hear the wind rushing and roaring in their long thick branches.

Heidi had a happy life. Every day in the summer she went up the mountain with Peter, the young goatherd. She knew the names of all the flowers, and she was friends with all the goats in Peter's herd.

In the wintertime, Heidi stayed inside at home with Grandfather, and watched him carve round wooden spoons, or hammer together chairs or tables.

Sometimes, Peter struggled up the snowy mountain path to call for Heidi, and took her down to visit his mother and his blind grandmother.

One day, Heidi's aunt came to take her to school.

So off went Heidi to Frankfurt far away.

Heidi soon made friends in Frankfurt. There
was the good old doctor who came to see Heidi's
cousin Clara, and who never left without saying
a kind word to Heidi.

There was Clara's grandmother, who taught
Heidi to read.

And of course there was Clara herself, pretty and sweet, but so pale and frail, and unable to walk or stand.

Heidi told her over and over again about Grandfather and Peter and the merry goats and the great fir trees. "Oh, if only you could go there," Heidi would say sadly. "You'd see, you would grow well and learn to walk there. Oh, if only we were home!"

Poor Heidi! She was so homesick for her mountains, with the green valley spreading below. Here in Frankfurt, even from the golden steeple of the church which she visited one day, as far as her eyes reached she could see only the gray stone houses of the city.

Many weeks went by, and every day Heidi grew paler and more homesick.

The kind old doctor who came to see Clara
spoke gravely to Mr. Sesemann, Clara's father.

"Heidi has grown thin and pale with home-
sickness. You must send her home at once, or she
will be very ill," he said.

The very next day Heidi's bag was packed so she could go back to the mountains she loved.

Heidi and Clara cried when they had to leave each other. "But just wait," Heidi said. "You will come to visit us soon, and then you will see how beautiful it is. And you will get well and strong up in the mountains!"

And then it was not long before Heidi was running up the path she knew so well, up to Grandfather's hut. Before Grandfather had seen her coming, she had thrown her arms around his neck.

"Grandfather!" she cried. "Grandfather! I am home and will never leave again!"

Heidi had to run out to see the goats, to hear the wind in the fir trees.

She had to hurry down the mountain path to Peter's grandmother, who wept with joy to find that Heidi could read to her now.

And every day, at least six times a day, she said to her grandfather, "We must bring Clara up here. Here Clara will get well and strong."

Heidi had her way at last. And one day a little procession wound up the mountain. Clara, well wrapped in shawls and blankets, was being carried up in a chair. Her father, carrying more warm shawls, followed behind.

"I am going to stay with you!" Clara told Heidi, her soft blue eyes shining. "I am going to stay with you and Grandfather and Peter and the goats for four whole weeks! Then Father will come back for me!"

Heidi could do nothing but hop for joy.

Every day after that Grandfather carried
Clara up where Peter kept his goats. He put her
down on the warm sweet grass, and then Heidi
would pick flowers for her friend, or sit beside
her to tell her the names of all the different
goats.

Every day Clara drank great bowlfuls of sweet goat milk. "This is so good," she sighed, "and I am so hungry! At home I never like to eat!"

"It is the healthy mountain air," smiled Grandfather.

By the time Mr. Sesemann came up to call for his little girl, instead of a pale invalid, he found a tall, smiling, rosy-cheeked Clara, who came walking toward him on Heidi's arm.

Mr. Sesemann ran up and clasped her in his arms. "How is this possible!" he cried. "How is this possible!"

And Heidi kept dancing around them both, singing happily, "I knew the mountains would make you well! I knew they would make you well!"